Turning the Tide

By

Mike Beckett

Table of Contents

Dedication

To my Granddaughters – Alice and Lucy.

Acknowledgements

For the support of my family, as I'm sure that there were times when my writing was not as smooth as they would have liked!

About the Author

Mike has been writing a monthly feature for a local magazine for over eighteen years, but this is his first novella. The idea for the story derives from a long-held belief that harnessing the power of the sea – and other water sources - could provide a major breakthrough for a sustainable source of electricity.

Chapter 1

Every so often, there comes a time that you will probably never, ever forget, and hopefully, it will be something that just catches all those good emotions and feelings – something that, when you look back, will still amaze you.

This was just the feeling that Rachel Andersen got on that beautiful summer evening as she sat in her garden overlooking the North Devon coastline. This was the house that she grew up in, the house that she loved so much, the house that helped her to eventually fulfil a part of her life that she never believed would actually happen. This is a story about the love of the sea and a challenge that grew in Rachel Andersen's mind.

Rachel was only three years old when her mother died tragically in a car accident. She was the only child of Alistair and Elaine Andersen and was brought up by her father as a single parent. Ever since she was born, Rachel and her dad were the best of friends, sharing life's difficulties but always looking after each other. Remarkably, this didn't stop as Rachel progressed her life in the usual pattern of good days bad days, discarding old boyfriends and meeting new ones.

One part of her life never changed: her love for the sea and all it contained. Living as they did on the coast, Rachel was an excellent swimmer and pretty good at surfing which pleased her dad as he had been a surfing champion in his day and still loved to show off his skills. But Rachel also loved exploring under the water and, by joining a local Scuba Club, soon became proficient.

Alistair Andersen had trained in engineering and eventually created his own business in repairing and restoring vehicles – usually older ones that had seen better days or were potentially collectors' items. But there was another side to Alistair that took up most of his spare time – that of being an inventor. It fascinated him that by looking at something in a different light and introducing a novel way of creating an invention, he frequently produced some winning designs. But this was not for the market – these inventions were done for his personal satisfaction and frequently ended up in storage.

During the early days of her upbringing, Rachel spent a lot of time with Alistair in his garage workshop. This started because Alistair wanted to spend as much time as he could with his daughter, so having her with him during the day was a real bonus for him. This time was also fascinating for Rachel, who began to develop a real interest in her dad's work. Although she never really aspired to become a motor engineer or mechanic, she did take a keen interest in the workings of engines, hydraulics and computer-managed systems. Maybe the best description would be that of a tomboy - although she also had a very feminine side to her. She also followed her dad in that area of curiosity, wanting to know how things worked and what made them tick. So, they made a great team and enjoyed their working environment together.

As time moved on, so did Rachel, as she established herself at the University of Southampton, studying engineering and oceanography. Although initially missing her dad and her friends, Rachel immersed herself in her studies and at the same time made new friends, including a boyfriend, Peter, who quite coincidentally lived fairly close to Rachel's home in North Devon.

Applying after graduating for various positions with companies and organisations operating in the areas that Rachel felt most drawn to, she was eventually offered a position with a coastal survey firm with their Head Office based in Penzance. Her role initially was working out of Penzance, as she learned just how they operated and how she would fit in with the business. Later, she travelled to their regional offices, spending time understanding the different projects that the company was running and getting to know about Britain's coastline and the sea in general.

Chapter 2

During one of her visits to a regional office on the Durham coast, Rachel fell on some slippery rocks and sprained her right ankle quite badly. Unable to drive, she was forced to spend time recuperating and working remotely while her ankle healed. This was when her thoughts turned towards what would turn out to be a major challenge. Her love and respect for the sea moved her to think about the ways that this powerful force that nature provided could be utilised. Her thoughts began to form into a plan – one that Rachel could see herself becoming absorbed in and one that she was beginning to feel would be really worthwhile, with a positive outcome.

In a nutshell, Rachel was pretty sure that there was a way of harnessing the power of the sea and producing electricity in a more efficient and greener way than was currently being achieved. So, while she was convalescing, Rachel began her research into her new project, and what she found only served to make her even more determined to follow her plan. Throughout her life Rachel had always been methodical in her ways of dealing with things, no matter what was involved. This, she was sure, came from her dad, and the way he solved problems with the vehicles he repaired and how he approached his latest invention. So, she set about her research by aligning two columns – the pros and cons of tidal power.

From the start, her pros list was always going to be greater than the cons. Otherwise, there would be no point in continuing. The sea provided a powerful source of energy with four predictable tides every day. It was a clean form of energy with no greenhouse gases and no requirement of fuel costs to generate this energy. Experts had estimated that 80% of tidal energy could be converted into electricity

- far more efficient than other sources – and could even produce around 11% of the UK's electricity requirement. The current turbines had a much longer life than either wind turbines or solar panels. Also, the turbines are at their most efficient point when used in shallow water, closer to the shore. This, of course, would also mean easier access for any routine maintenance.

Rachel's list of cons included a possibly higher cost of establishing each unit and maybe a limited number of suitable locations. There could be some environmental impact, and the sea is highly corrosive. She also discovered that currently, there are only four tidal power sites in the UK, so it didn't appear that there was a huge interest in taking it further.

However, Rachel was not in the least daunted by her research, but rather it had increased her desire to dig deeper into ways that this 'dream' could become a reality. She confided in her dad, who also was intrigued by the idea of utilising this freely available energy source – his inventive brain was already starting to move into gear.

"I think that what we need to look at are the ways that we can copy the act of the current sea turbine to produce something that has the fewest moving parts encased in a completely sealed compartment and uses materials that have extremely long working lives," mused Rachel.

"Not much to ask, then!" replied Alistair.

While Alistair put on his thinking cap, Rachel began making a study of Britain's coastline, concentrating on the tides, and looking for potential sites. Again, experts had suggested that places like the Isle of Wight and the Bristol Channel had particularly strong tides throughout the year.

While these tidal power generators would not be visible once installed, there would still be some disruption with bringing this power onto the mainland, albeit minimal when compared to other sources of energy.

But Rachel did not just concentrate on how this project could become a commercially viable operation, she also dug deep into the competitor market. How expensive was it to build wind turbines out at sea? What sort of annual maintenance costs are involved? What effect do they have on sea life, shipping and other environmental concerns? She did the same calculation for solar panels and dug deeply into the cost of nuclear power as well as fossil fuels. The more involved she became, the more she began to believe that there must be an answer in harnessing tidal Britain. Perhaps for the first time in her life, Rachel knew what it meant when she remembered the phrase - 'my brain hurts!' Intense concentration requires a break every so often – a time to recharge the batteries and freshen thoughts.

Chapter 3

But Rachel's brain was only just starting to put together some new thoughts about tidal power, and she decided it was time to run them past her dad. So that evening, she and Alistair sat down to go through the ideas that were running around Rachel's head.

"What I thought was this," began Rachel. "When you introduce a flow of water through a narrow orifice and set this inside another tube, you will create a vortex that will draw other water from outside the vortex tube and along the tube that contains it."

"So, what does that achieve?" asked Alistair. "Apart from drawing more water along the tube."

"Ah, but what you also do is affix rows of small turbines along the carrier tube, and these will be activated by this new water force created by the vortex," explained Rachel.

"You could have something there," admitted Alistair, who was now becoming increasingly interested in what could be a commercially viable system. Excited by this possibility, the pair started to put together a potential working model – in plan form – and look more closely at each individual unit.

Alistair suggested that he may have a novel way of mounting the turbine's moving parts – a way that reduced the potential stress and wear of the normal method being currently used. This, combined with the use of a sealing compound that he had already tried in an earlier experiment that required the total waterproofing of underwater lighting, might just give them a viable unit. It would be lightweight but tough, totally sealed for long-life protection and relatively inexpensive to produce in volume.

If all this came together, there could be a system that would be secured to the seabed, with each unit housing maybe twelve turbines and mounted on a 360-degree turntable that would be controlled by a sensor that would cater to facing the four tides every day. Choosing just where these power producers were to be sited would require careful planning. Initially, Alistair and Rachel wanted to produce the first prototype and trial it somewhere that replicated the unit's eventual home.

"I think we could persuade David over at the Bratton Watermill to let us use the water flow just after his mill race," suggested Alistair. "It is wide enough to provide a fairly fast flow of water, and it's also totally private. We could monitor it from here using CCTV as well as making regular visits to check on performance."

That evening, Rachel, Alistair and Peter dropped in at their local pub to enjoy a well-earned drink and discuss their project further. Although Peter was not directly involved, he was as enthusiastic as the other two. He enjoyed researching the UK coastline, taking on the role of finding out where the best sitings might be once they had approved the unit to be commercially viable. Important factors included those parts of the coastline that offered strong tidal currents with minimal impact on the environment, tourism and wildlife. They must also allow access to the units once positioned and a way of directing the power to a suitable land site without causing disruption or incurring heavy costs.

They all agreed that if this was going to be easy, then it would have been done already, and they would be just another company competing in a large market. Still, this did not deter the trio as they continued with their plans.

For the next few weeks, Rachel was back at work and could only help her dad at weekends. Alistair, too, needed to keep his workshop going – not least because their project would require considerable funding, particularly if it did prove to be successful. But progress was being made, and eventually the first prototype was constructed. They decided to give it a temporary name of "The Alirach Turbine" – (to be properly titled when they were happy that it was a viable proposition) but taking a part of each of their first names.

Chapter 4

After several weeks of intense planning, cutting, welding, moulding and buckets of perspiration, the prototype was ready for trialling at Bratton Watermill after getting permission from the owner, David. Securing the unit with a suitable anchorage proved more difficult than they imagined, but they finally managed it, and from above, it was barely visible. They planned to forward the power from Alirach to storage batteries inside one of the Watermill's outbuildings, where they could monitor performance. Despite their research, neither Alistair nor Rachel had really worked out what output they could expect. They had the readings from the turbine manufacturer, but Alistair had altered it, and consequently, it could not now conform to the original specification.

Around 2.15 that afternoon, an apprehensive trio waited as Alirach was switched on. Of course, it was somewhat of a letdown initially, as nothing was visible or could be heard when it started running. The only indication would be seen by watching the monitoring unit that would be registering the amount of power being generated – if any! Alistair had linked in an ammeter to record the current, and the results were also downloaded to a computer. This enabled the reading of whatever was being produced to be available for checking at any time and would show the highs and lows during any period selected. They had all agreed that they would do one check at the start-up and then no more for a period of twelve hours.

Rachel had already decided that, at this point, she only really wanted to have some indication – hopefully a fairly strong one – that what they were trying to achieve did have a future. She knew that they were minute fish in a world of giant whales, and their knowledge and resources were very limited when compared to those companies trying to achieve the same objective. But there was a "David and Goliath" feeling about this challenge, and it would take more than an initial setback to stop her determination.

After the previously mentioned twelve hours had passed, the trio decided to check on the progress – if any! However, they were pleasantly surprised to find that there were, indeed, readings showing that Alirach had achieved some power. Not as much as they had hoped, but certainly enough to boost their morale and prompt them to have a further discussion on what they should next concentrate on for the next stage. Alistair said that he would like to look further into the workings of the turbine – the manner in which it was driven, the type of blade or propeller that turned the shaft – because he felt that there could be greater efficiency from the unit if he could devise a more effective mechanism, one that could increase the energy performance with less wear and tear on the moving parts.

Rachel, however, was torn between two possible thoughts on the project. Should their aim still be to look at tidal power around Britain's coast? Or would it make more sense to concentrate on internal waterways by utilising smaller, more cost-effective Alirachs? These could be produced for the market that required sufficient electricity for a smaller, local use, using water from streams, rivers and waterfalls. Then, power could be provided for heating, lighting, cooking and domestic appliances on a more achievable basis. But this still relied on the efficiency of the Alirach unit, which Alistair wanted to upgrade, enabling it to produce more than it was currently showing.

Time passed as Rachel, Alistair and Peter steadily worked on their respective jobs yet still pursuing their ideas on waterpower. Then, a potential breakthrough came as Alistair found a way of building a turbine that used fewer moving parts and also required less waterpower to produce even more amperage. But as these were still early days, Alistair didn't want to explain just what he had constructed. He felt that if this were as successful as he anticipated, then it would need protection. The first stage of this protection would be to keep the new construction a complete secret. He was not sure if it was eligible for a patent, but he felt that it was worth keeping under wraps for the time being. What he was fairly sure about was that his research had not found another system that was remotely like this one, so it was worth saying little until they had put it into practice and proved that it really did work.

The three got together to decide the next phase for what had now become Alirach 2. After much discussion, Rachel agreed that if Alistair's latest version did perform well, then concentrating on internal water sources rather than coastal tides may be the best plan. The final decision would be made after they had conducted trials and learned more about the potential power that could be generated by Alirach 2.

"I've been thinking about our trial area for Alirach 2," said Alistair. "I think that we should look for another source – maybe this time a river or fast-flowing stream?"

"Why do you want to move? We know it has potential at the Mill," countered Rachel.

"I just feel that using another source would give us another statistic – hopefully in our favour – and more proof of the markets that we are looking for," replied Alistair.

"We could try the River Farbeck, then take off from the Taw," said Peter. "It has a fast-flowing stretch that runs through my uncle's farm, and I'm sure he would let us use it for our trial."

They all agreed that this would be beneficial and Peter was designated with the job of persuading his uncle. As he had predicted, there wasn't a problem – especially when there could be a potential power source for the farm.

The team visited the site, and a suitable spot was found to secure Alirach 2 and house the CCTV and storage batteries. This all took time as it could only be carried out at weekends, and adverse weather conditions delayed their work even further. But eventually they managed to set everything in place, and the next phase of their project began.

Much to Alistair's surprise and delight, Alirach 2 produced quite a lot more power than the first unit. This pleased Alistair as the flow at this site was not as strong as at the Mill race, yet it was more productive.

"I think we are going the right way," he told Rachel and Peter. "Concentrating on smaller, more effective units looks to be paying off. If we can move a little further along these lines, then we may be able to consider what a commercial line would entail."

But at the back of his mind was the sheer cost of what this next step could amount to – and the funding that he had available would not be sufficient. At the same time, Rachel was also considering what could happen next if all went really well. So, she decided to do further research into two sources – one would be companies who were already operating in this area, and the other might be those organisations involved in capital ventures. She readily admitted that the world of finance was not her forte, but she wanted an insight that would at least give her some background into the way things worked.

Whilst Alirach 2 was continuing to happily produce energy 24/7 and build up a comfortable amount of battery storage, Alistair worked on the fine-tuning that he felt was needed before looking into commercial units. This entailed checking the materials used, the waterproof coating, which was so obviously important, the life of the moving parts and so on. As he worked through each detail, he realised that he was becoming more and more excited by the prospect of what they were doing. Alistair had never been given to fantasy or ever got really carried away by any of his previous inventions, but this one was giving him a buzz that was new to him. It wasn't the possibility of making money out of it but much more the idea that he could have hit on something that actually made a lot of sense and could make so much difference to many people. He still hadn't forgotten Rachel's original idea of harnessing the tides, and he often wondered if he should spend time looking further into that potential for power production.

Chapter 5

However, there was a change in Rachel's life when her company asked her to attend an Ocean Preservation Conference that was being held in Paris over three days. Of course, she was thrilled to be asked as her love of the sea, and all connections with it were so important to her. But while she was there, she also took advantage of being able to seek out those commercial operations that may have some interest in Alirach2. Near the end of the second day, she picked out a Swiss company that was developing a line of centrifugal pumps for use in diverting water courses and for large-quantity transfer systems. Although this was not a direct connection to tidal turbines, she thought that there might be some mutual benefit in a joint enterprise. After talking to one of the sales staff, she found herself explaining her project to the owner, who initially did not seem to be particularly interested. But as they continued talking about the possible benefits to both sides, there was a change of heart, and the idea of a potential collaboration began to form.

Rachel left with an agreement that Josef Karlsen – the owner – would visit the Alirach 2 trial site to look further into what could be jointly done. That evening, Rachel spent her time researching the Swiss company to learn more about their operation, finances, history and so forth. She also rang Alistair and told him of her suggestion and about the potential meeting. Naturally, Alistair was a little surprised at the suddenness of Rachel's idea but did agree that it was worth exploring.

The visit, by Josef Karlsen – who also brought along his chief development officer – proved to be well worth the time spent examining Alirach2 and discussing what could be good for both parties. Karlsen explained that his company, although not large, was involved in projects in several European countries. They mainly concentrated on the movement of water – either for short-term transfer or for permanent applications. And, yes, that did involve rivers, streams and watercourses where the potential use of Alirach 2 may well have a place. The interest by both sides was growing and it was agreed that Alistair and Rachel would pay a visit to the Swiss factory the following weekend.

The visit went well, and Alistair and Rachel were impressed with what they saw inside Josef's factory. Clean, well-run, busy and equally important, the people that they met seemed to enjoy working there and were happy to talk about their work. However, upon their return home to North Devon, there was a disturbing message from Peter's uncle.

It appeared that there had been a break-in at the farm, and Alirach 2, along with all associated equipment, had been taken. They were devastated. As far as they knew, nobody else was aware of what they were doing there other than Peter's uncle, who they trusted completely. Everything that they had achieved, built up, modified, fine-tuned, and spent hours and hours working on had now disappeared. But what really shocked them was the fact that nothing else was taken. There were many valuable pieces of farm equipment, tools, welding equipment and access to a very well-stocked workshop, but nothing else had been touched. This must mean that someone had specifically entered the farm with the sole intent of taking Alirach 2.

That evening, they gathered together to talk about this massive blow to their project. They had all been totally absorbed with Alirach 2 but had not considered what they should have done to protect themselves from exactly what had occurred. It was doubtful that any insurance policy that Alistair might have would offer any cover. There appeared to be no evidence of an obvious intruder/thief that they could see.

"I must ask Peter's uncle if anyone else could have known what we are doing on the farm," said Alistair.

"And don't forget to also ask if his stockman, George, has any ideas," added Rachel.

The following morning, Alistair caught up with Peter's uncle, John Denhill, and asked his questions.

"No, I haven't said a word to anyone – I do know how important it is to you to have these trials under wraps," said John. "I would ask George, but he has left me and gone back to his family in Germany. Decided he needed to be back home – I think he was planning to do that next year, when he was due to retire, but decided to go now rather than later. Left me with a bit of a work gap and until I can replace him, I'm having to pay through the nose for a temporary stockman."

"When did this happen?" asked Alistair.

"The Friday evening before you left for Switzerland," replied John.

"Do you have an address or contact number for him?" asked Alistair. "I would like to ask him if he saw anything unusual before he left."

"I've got it somewhere back at the house – I'll forward it to you when I get back at lunchtime," promised John.

Alistair was somewhat puzzled by what John had told him about George. He didn't really have much to do with the stockman, so he couldn't really form an opinion. However, it did seem convenient that he had suddenly upped sticks and left for Germany. It also looked a little strange that no other clues were showing that anyone else had been around – or was he just grasping at straws?

That evening, over supper, Alistair told Rachel and Peter of his conversation with John, and how he was a little uneasy with the sudden disappearance of George. Although there was no real evidence to link him with the space left by Alirach 2, the fact that nothing else had been touched and there didn't appear to be any sign of forced entry was rather odd. Should they get the police involved? Would the publicity have an adverse effect on their project – bringing out into the open just what they were trying to keep quiet? Also, apart from the actual equipment, what had they lost?

Alistair received a text from John giving the details that he had about George. He had hired George Barker four years ago, and even though he was not a young man, he came with a creditable background as a stockman. He lived locally in a flat – a single man but with a wife and son in Germany. The only detail that John was able to offer was that the town in Germany was called Straustern, somewhere not far from Berlin. He thought that the family name was Klasmann, but that was all he could give to Alistair.

Alistair scoured maps and pored over the internet, looking for names and places, but found little of value. What he did discover was that there was a town east of Berlin called Strausberg – the nearest place he could find with a similar name - but he had no luck in finding people with names like Klasmann. Without spending money on using a private investigator, Alistair decided that this may all be for nothing

– maybe George had even moved elsewhere for whatever reason, and the German connection – and possibly the family – were simply red herrings.

What was playing at the back of Alistair's mind was the possibility of his invention being in the hands of a company that could produce it under their name. If this did happen, unless he could actually find such a unit and strip it down and prove that it was his design, there would be no way that he would ever know. This was probably taking things too far, so his thoughts turned back to closer to home.

Chapter 6

Their first tests were carried out in the waters of David Bratton's Watermill. Alistair didn't know David that well – they didn't really move in the same circles, and David didn't spend that much time at the Watermill. Most of the week was spent in London, where he was a partner in a furniture company, specialising in a 'working-from-home' design of office furniture. This was seemingly successful as there had been an enormous move from offices to people working from their own houses. Was there some connection here? When Alistair switched from the Watermill to the farm for his second testing area, David was not entirely happy as he had been using the benefits from the power provided by Alirach, and now this was no longer available. Surely, this was not sufficient reason for him to sabotage Alistair and Rachel's plans, was it? Or did he simply take it back to his mill, thereby providing himself with free power once again?

This thought persisted with Alistair, and he wondered if the only solution would be to go back to the Watermill - on some pretext that he might have left some parts behind – and prove that this was just in his mind and had no relevance.

So, he got together with Rachel and Peter and told them of his thoughts. Peter felt that there could be something in this theory and made a suggestion to them that might just help prove Alistair right or not.

"My uncle uses a drone on his farm – it helps look for a wide range of subject matter, like the lack of nitrogen, sulphate or potassium in his crops. He also uses it for detecting broken drainage pipes, and what's even more relevant is that it can detect electricity lines and power cables. So, if we direct it over the spot where we trialled Alirach, then we would know if it had been replaced and was back in use, again, for the watermill's power supply," enthused Peter.

"But how close do we need to be to operate the drone and direct it to the exact spot?" asked Rachel.

"Not a problem – it uses a camera so that wherever the operator is based, he can steer the unit to exactly where he wants it - even at night. Using night flight technology, he can clearly see the terrain," reassured Peter.

The trio continued to discuss the potential of using the drone to check out whether Alirach was back at the watermill and just how risky it would be. In the end, they decided that the best time would be in daylight when David was in London, and the watermill was quiet. The drone could be operated from a short distance away from the actual spot in the mill race where Alirach had been situated – making doubly sure that they were picking up the power from this unit and not from another source.

The following day, Peter announced that he wouldn't be able to help them for a few days. It appeared that his grandfather had had a bad fall in his home near Edinburgh and needed help with his smallholding as he would not be able to walk for a while. Peter was the only member of the family who was in a position to provide this help and, so, left the same day to take over the required duties. Happily, John Denhill said that he would be pleased to step in for Peter while he was away and run the drone over the watermill race to check out what was taking place – if anything.

But that evening, Alistair had a phone call from John asking him if he could call round – something was not as it should be, and he wanted to talk with Alistair and Rachel.

"I rang James – Peter's grandfather – to find out just what had happened and how badly injured he was from the fall," said John, "but he hadn't a clue what I was talking about. He is as fit as a fiddle, hasn't had a fall and has not seen or heard from Peter for a long time...!"

This news totally confused John, and both Alistair and Rachel couldn't work out what Peter was doing, and why did he suddenly decide to vanish.

"You know what we should do immediately?" said Alistair. "Go straight up to Bratton Watermill and check if Alirach is there – or not."

"Are you thinking that Peter has vanished, taking Alirach with him?" asked an astonished Rachel.

Alistair admitted that this was a possibility even though he really hoped that it was not the case, but actually seeing for themselves if Bratton Watermill did or did not have the turbine would at least rule out one factor in this mystery.

The visit to the watermill proved that there was no sign of Alirach 2 and no evidence that anything had changed since they had left and moved their equipment up to the farm. In one respect, both Alistair and Rachel had hoped that the turbine would be there, meaning that it was unlikely that Peter was involved. But it also pointed a finger at Peter – the fact that both Peter and Alirach 2 had vanished at the same time.

Chapter 7

That evening, Alistair and Rachel went over and over the events of the last few days. Although Peter was indeed Rachel's boyfriend, their relationship hadn't flourished as much as Alistair had expected, and she didn't seem as worried about Peter's leaving so abruptly as she did about the loss of Alirach 2. However, she did admit to her dad that things had been 'quieter' between them, but that didn't appear to be troubling her as much as Alistair thought it would.

"I think I had better ring Josef Karlsen," said Alistair, "and explain what has happened so far as we know. This may well end any arrangement that we had hoped to make with his company." Rachel agreed, and the call was made.

Josef was very understanding about what had happened. He asked Alistair if he thought that Peter might have been making contacts with companies that were already producing water turbines with a view to doing some sort of a deal. But Alistair wasn't certain that Peter had sufficient understanding of just how Alirach 2 was constructed or even what were the actual materials used in the build. It was something that only Alistair knew, and he hadn't even documented the development. Of course, this also meant that there was no printed literature or plans that could be removed from Alistair's workshop – it all remained inside Alistair's head. When Josef asked what Alistair planned to do next, he was surprised that Alistair said that he hadn't really thought any further than finding out what had happened to Alirach 2.

However, Josef suggested that if he did decide to start again and construct Alirach 3, then he would still be interested in a joint venture.

"If it would help in any way, I would be very happy to offer you the use of my facilities here," he told Alistair. "We have room for you, and I would think pretty much all the equipment that you probably require."

Alistair was delighted to hear of Josef's offer and told him that he would discuss it with Rachel and would get back to him as soon as they had talked. What Alistair did know was that he really did want to create Alirach 3 – the trial results so far were more than encouraging. He regarded the loss of Alirach 2 as nothing more than just another problem to deal with. Rachel was equally delighted to hear what Josef had offered. After a lengthy discussion, they both agreed that it made sense to go ahead with this opportunity. After all, it was probably what might have happened if the current problems had not taken place.

The next few weeks flew by as Alistair decided to move temporarily to Switzerland and begin the construction of Alirach 3. With the assistance of Josef's chief designer there were some changes made, both with materials being used and with further design development that could provide the turbine with even greater efficiency. They also put forward a request to the Patent Office, hoping that they could get some protection with the way that this particular turbine operated. However, this would take some time, and they would have to be patient and wait for the results.

There was also another change – Alistair, Rachel and Josef set up a joint company specifically for Alirach 3 and any further products that may be relevant. The name that they decided upon was Alirach Turbo Power Limited, or ATPOL for short. One of the reasons for doing this was a suggestion by Rachel that her original idea for sea-driven, tidal turbines could still be a possibility. This also appealed to

Josef, who agreed that they should seriously consider this as a project once Alirach 3 had proved to be commercially viable.

Rachel busied herself with her coastal survey work, also enjoying her time visiting their various project sites around the UK coast. She used this as a way of checking out possible venues for the tidal sea turbine project that she hoped would one day come to fruition. Although Peter's whereabouts did cross her mind quite often, she was more disappointed than upset by his sudden departure and possible theft of Alirach 2. At times, there was a feeling of anger that she had never suspected that anything of this nature would take place, reminding her that she hadn't known Peter as well as she had thought. As time passed, and there was no contact of any sort from him, she slowly began to put this episode behind her and get on with what could be a really exciting period where her vision of turning the tide into an actual reality could possibly happen.

Alistair stayed in Switzerland long enough for Alirach 3 to be built and put out for trials in a water course not far from Josef's factory. He was happy to leave collecting of information to Josef and his team and returned home to catch up with his work, which was already building up a backlog. Although he was in daily contact with Rachel, there was still much to discuss on his return. They had established a three-way communication link with Josef that was pretty secure and kept one another abreast of what was happening with Alirach 3 and the ongoing test results.

Both Alistair and Rachel were really happy with what they were hearing from Josef, and it looked as if there was every chance of commercial trials being set up with a small number of selected users. These would be situated in an area within close access to the Swiss factory for ease of record-taking, and the Swiss engineers could easily handle any maintenance or troubleshooting.

Then, a few days later, Alistair received a telephone call that he certainly had not been expecting. The caller introduced himself as Alex Warner and explained that he was the CEO of a company called AquaTurb – a manufacturer of turbines based in the north of Britain. He was ringing to ask Alistair if he could call in later that day as he wanted to show him something that could be of interest. Alistair hadn't heard of the company but was intrigued to know more, and so agreed to meet up in the afternoon. He Googled AquaTurb and discovered that it was, indeed, a company involved in water turbines. This set Alistair's mind wondering if Alex had heard of what Alistair was doing and maybe there was some interest.

The afternoon turned out to be a little different than the thoughts that Alistair was having. Having explained what his company produced, he then took Alistair out to his car and opened the boot to show him something that he thought might be of interest. What he looked at was his very own Alirach 2, the one that had vanished from their trials in the River Farbeck. Alistair was astonished and naturally wanted to know how this came into Alex's hands.

It seemed that Peter and George had called Alex's company and suggested that they might like to have a joint venture in the production of Alirach 2 as they had all the required facilities to build it. In contrast, Peter and George were only the inventors. However, Alex began to be suspicious during his conversation with Peter as the answers to some of the questions that he put to them were not at all credible. The more he delved into it, the more he realised that the pair only had limited knowledge about the product that they claimed was their invention. So, feigning an interest, he suggested that they leave the unit with him for a few days, and then he would get back to them with a plan. He became more suspicious when Peter only left him with a mobile number and wouldn't provide an address where he could be contacted. Then, of course, his own contacts within the turbine industry soon turned up some details about Alistair's experiment – there is always someone who knows something. Eventually, he managed to get Alistair's telephone number.

After hearing Alex's account, Alistair told him what he was doing without giving away all the facts and figures. Alex was quite understanding and told Alistair that if things didn't work out as planned, perhaps he would consider talking again to him about any help that he may be able to offer. The one factor that Alistair felt that suggested that Alex was being fair and honest was that Alirach2 was still completely intact, and had not been tampered with or stripped down. The original seals were still in place, and none of the securing plates and bolts showed any sign of being touched. Naturally, he was delighted with this turn of events and immediately updated Rachel and Josef with the news.

The next question was what to do, if anything, about Peter and George. The mobile number that Alex had for Peter was different from the one that Alistair had, so obviously, he had changed it to be sure that Alistair or Rachel could not contact him.

That evening Alistair and Rachel sat down to decide what they felt should happen next with Peter and George. Rachel said that she really had no feelings for Peter and would be quite happy if this was now an end to that particular period of her life. Alistair admitted that he didn't think that there was a lot of point in chasing the pair of them – after all, what could they do that might jeopardise the future of Alirach 3? They had no drawings, no unit to offer competitors and certainly insufficient information about the actual workings of the turbine. After further discussion, they both decided to leave matters as they were and do nothing unless Peter and George cropped up somewhere else, which seemed very unlikely. Alex had told Alistair that he would be contacting Peter and informing him of his meeting with Alistair and that Alirach 2 was back with the rightful owners. It would be very unlikely that either Peter or George would show up and risk being charged with, at least, theft of equipment.

Chapter 8

Alistair and Rachel returned to Switzerland and were delighted to find that Josef had four more Alirach3 units out on commercial trials. All were working extremely well and producing excellent returns of electricity – more than Alistair had predicted. Josef confessed that his design team had slightly changed two parts of the turbine – one was the use of a different material for the blades, and the other was a design change in the shape of the blades. When Josef explained just what they had done, Alistair was in total agreement, and wondered why he hadn't also looked more closely at the blade design as the new configuration made so much more sense. Josef had also been very busy ensuring that the records were accurate and that each of the four units was regularly checked and operating as designed. The plan was that these commercial tests would be closely monitored for six months, and if all proved to be as it should be, then they would consider offering them on the market to potential customers.

Once this was agreed, Alistair and Rachel returned to England and back to their respective work. They really could do nothing more to help with Alirach 3, and the next few months would all be in the hands of Josef. The commercial sales got underway, and it soon became clear that there was a pretty strong call for such a unit. Once word got around, the market reacted, and the sales grew.

Time passed quite quickly, and Alistair immersed himself in his own backlog of work that had built up while Rachel had been promoted and was now in charge of external projects for her company. This involved much more travel around the UK but also gave her the opportunity to still inspect potential sites for her tidal dream. At the back of her mind, she still believed that harnessing the daily tides could have an excellent role in the future of Alirach and the "free" sourcing of electricity.

As she sat in her garden looking at the glorious open sea, glinting in the evening sun, she pondered further over what had happened over the last years. All the work that had been put into the design and development of Alirach, all the testing that they had carried out and despite the sudden loss of their second unit, how fate had given them another chance with the birth of Alirach 3. Alistair joined her, bringing with him a glass of wine each.

"Dad, I know that you've mentioned a couple of times that it was probably time that you thought about retiring and taking life at a slower pace, but before you do, I've got a little idea for you." put in Rachel.

"Why am I getting the impression that this is anything but little?" queried Alistair.

"O.K. – all I want you to do is this. Just write down for me all the forms of powered watercraft that you can think of, all the forms of powered land vehicles and the same for the sky," said Rachel.

"Why?" asked Alistair simply.

"Well, why are we going to the rivers, streams, watercourses and so on when we should be taking Alirach to them? We have been thinking of putting in a static version when there is a massive market out there for a mobile Alirach! Just imagine a version that could be fitted – either as an add-on or as part of a new build – to every potential water-propelled unit, an air turbine to every land-powered vehicle and the same for anything that flies!" said an excited Rachel. "We could also look at fitting it to all forms of powered water supplies

– main water supplies to houses, shops, factories, hospitals – anywhere that receives a flow of water. What do you think?"

Chapter 9

Alistair was stunned, but his brain was ticking and beginning to see just where Rachel's thoughts had taken her.

"You know, you might just have hit on something that could dramatically change so much in the world," said Alistair.

He was already thinking about other countries and how their sources of both water and air could also be harnessed to power turbines and generate electricity by Alirach. It would require considerable changes in the specification of Alirach if those many areas of use that were springing to mind were to be accommodated. But this was going to need a tremendous amount of work – and a lot more technical help than Alistair could muster, even with his inventive brain. In just under a week's time, Josef was due to arrive for their usual quarterly Board Meeting, so Alistair suggested to Rachel that they prepare something to put forward at this meeting with the idea that could start the ball rolling with this potentially global plan.

That evening, Rachel and Alistair sat down – literally with pen and paper – to gather their thoughts and formulate a plan that they could put to Josef. There would be an addition to the Board of ATPOL as Josef's son, Daniel, who had been training with a hydro-power company for the last few years and now was joining his father's company. Alistair had met him on previous visits to Switzerland but this would be the first meeting for Rachel. What Alistair did know about Daniel was that he was very much like Josef, both in looks and disposition. Although quite tall, he gave the impression of having a "gentle giant" personality and Alistair was quite happy for him to be part of their team. What he didn't expect was the obvious mutual attraction that he witnessed when Daniel was introduced to Rachel!

The Board Meeting went well, with genuine enthusiasm from both Josef and Daniel about the potential impact that a mobile Alirach could have in an enormous market. The one factor that each person gathered around that table shared was the ability to always challenge whatever they were contemplating. So immediately, they asked each other why this project had not been done by any of the many companies that produced turbines. Had they missed something that was so obvious that it would make the whole idea unworkable? Perhaps they should consider making a short list of the major producers of turbines with a view to collaboration, and strangely enough, this viewpoint came from Josef, who felt that if this project was a feasible proposition, it might just be too big for his company to fulfil. However, there was concern this might take the whole project away from their control.

"Maybe there is something that we should consider before we decide to go further," said Alistair. "We have little or no protection for Alirach. Perhaps we should look at the possibility of taking out a patent on our unit – if, of course, this is possible."

"I would completely agree," put in Daniel, "as this is a far too important breakthrough to not have the protection that it deserves. I do have a contact at the Patent Office, so I will make some inquiries into the possibility of having a patent for Alirach."

Since the beginning of their association Josef had always stayed with Alistair and Rachel, and even with the addition of Daniel, the same arrangement continued. Because of the length of the agenda at their meeting, Alistair had arranged for them to have their evening meal at the local pub, and it did not surprise him that after they had finished the meal, he and Josef went back to the house, leaving Rachel and Daniel at the pub.

"I doubt that they are discussing the future of Alirach!" said Josef as they left the pub.

"Would you?" laughed Alistair.

The next few days passed quickly as Alistair and Josef spent their time working out the module that would form a mobile Alirach. Rachel and Daniel researched into the possibility of taking out a worldwide patent on Alirach. Apart from anything else, they knew that it would be expensive. Still, also that it would afford them protection for the next twenty years and if this were to be the global success that they anticipated, then it was absolutely right to spend money in this way.

However, there was a rather unpleasant surprise when they submitted their application to the Patent Office. They were informed that there already was an application pending that was too close to the one that they put forward so nothing could be granted at this stage. But even more devastating was the news that Peter Denhill had submitted the application pending.

Alistair and Rachel were stunned. Neither had given Peter another thought since the mystery of the lost Alirach had been cleared up. Rachel was particularly upset – mainly because she had not for one minute felt that he would take things any further than he already had done. Alistair was astonished that Peter had copied drawings and details of Alirach, which meant that he had rifled through Alistair's office, in order to be able to submit an application to the Patent Office.

The next few days saw a black cloud hanging over their heads, and what action should follow had to be decided quickly before Peter's application was granted. A meeting was arranged with John Denhill to ask for any help that he could give – particularly with reference to the taking of Alirach without permission from John's farm – that might provide further evidence as to the title of Alirach. John, of course, was only too happy to do this. So armed with as much evidence as they could put together, a meeting was arranged with the Patent Office.

What should have been a straightforward meeting turned out to be rather more difficult than expected. Apparently, Peter had anticipated that Alistair and Rachel might also try to take out a patent. So, he had engineered a scheme that would put Alistair et al in the position of the defrauding party who were attempting to gain a patent under false pretences. He had managed to provide evidence – stolen from Alistair – to show that he was the inventor, and although he worked alongside Alistair in the garage, he used the workshop to create Alirach. Peter also claimed that Alistair and Rachel were envious of his ability to produce such a unit and that they were trying to steal away the rights to the patent for their own purposes.

The discussions went on for some considerable time, but finally, the Patent Office agreed that the title to Alirach did indeed belong to the company ATPOL and that all claims by Peter Denhill were considered null and void. This was a great - relief even though they all knew that Peter's claim was completely false. But this wasn't the end of it, as the granting of a patent had yet to be confirmed, and this could take up to three years or more. However, this denoted that action had been taken and all they could do now was to get on with the next phase – at least with the knowledge that now could have some protection in the offing.

Back home, the four of them sat down to decide what, if anything, they should do about Peter. The first question at the back of all their minds was this. Did they think that he would try anything further? This was followed by - should we be taking any action against Peter? After much debate, they came to a decision that, for the time being, they would let things lie. It would be difficult, time consuming, costly and would probably not provide them with any real satisfaction if they attempted to bring about legal proceedings against Peter. They all agreed to put the matter behind them and concentrate on the next phase for Alirach.

Josef and Daniel returned to Switzerland after what had proved to be several 'interesting' days. The ups and downs that had followed each other in fairly rapid succession had come as surprises to both Josef and Daniel.

"I'm pleased about the potential for mobile Alirach," said Josef, "and I'm pleased that you are getting on so well with Rachel."

"Yes, both situations came as a surprise to me," replied Daniel. "I had no idea that Rachel would make such an impact – I really do like her. And the idea of producing a mobile Alirach is a terrific one." Watching his son closely, Josef detected a slight reddening of Daniel's cheeks when speaking of Rachel and smiled to himself.

The major conversation that took place between Josef and Daniel was the question of whether they should manufacture mobile Alirach themselves, or look at sub-contracting it. Although this would be a Board decision, Josef and Daniel had a majority shareholding and could make the final decision between them – if they had to. They both agreed that if the production did rise substantially the current factory had plenty of land around it upon which they could expand. If there were to be a problem it might be one of raising the money with which to expand their premises. But at the moment they were not in a position to make even an educated guess at which model would be first to take off, or what sort of quantities would be involved, and so on. Their conclusion was to continue with their present commitments and plan for the trials of the first mobile units as the decisions upon which market would be their first target.

Chapter 10

For the next few months everyone pressed on with their individual roles – Alistair with the design of a version of mobile Alirach that could be attached to small watercraft as this would be very similar to the already proven version that they had constructed. Also, the global market for this particular model was enormous and could become the mainstay of their business. The main difference would be in the way that it would be attached to the watercraft, and this should not be a major problem for Alistair. Once completed, tests followed using a company that hires out leisure craft in reasonably large numbers. It was decided that these tests should last for a period of eight weeks, with regular checks being carried out.

Meanwhile, Josef and Daniel had no problem in persuading the Board of Directors to take on this project – in fact, there was unanimous support as they could see not only potential job security for the workforce but additional manpower would be needed if all went well. On the financial side, there was also progress, albeit with some constraints. Josef's current bank was willing to provide finance, but there would need to be guarantees in the form of collateral - namely, the factory and Josef's own property and land.

Back in North Devon, Alistair and Rachel were busy, not only with the changes that were required with Alirach but also with the instruction manuals, publicity material and the marketing policy that would be essential for sales.

All was looking good until Alistair received a late phone call that brought him news that he didn't want to hear. It was Josef telling Alistair that there had been a fire at the factory. Although it was being contained, there was considerable damage to the area designated for the production of Alirach. Alistair and Rachel were devastated, hardly believing what Josef was telling them. After a short discussion I agreed Alistair would fly out immediately to the factory.

"You know, at the back of my mind, I can't help but think that this was not just an accident. Josef keeps that factory as if it were his front room. Everything was in the correct place, and all safety precautions are regularly checked. But, of course, I can only speculate from here – not the best way to direct my thoughts." said Alistair.

Alistair arrived to find that the fire had been completely extinguished, but not one person - except for Josef – was to be seen.

"As soon as the fire brigade had left, we had the insurance inspectors visit to determine how the fire began," explained Josef. "I have been questioned closely – more like an interrogation – to find out if I was having financial difficulties, or if I had enemies, or even if I had recently sacked anyone who may have had a grievance against me or the company. They are asking to see our latest accounts and are now spending time going through the damaged area with a fine toothcomb hoping to establish the reason why the fire started."

As they discussed this in greater detail, Josef did point out two things that were still playing around in his mind, and he felt that there was a connection that ought to shed some light. From the start of his business Josef had installed closed circuit television (CCTV) and had kept them well up to date as the technology advanced. All the CCTV cameras positioned around the area where the fire had taken place had been deliberately smashed, but others situated further along had not been touched. Also, if someone had really wanted to burn the factory down, they would have started at the opposite end where there was a large amount of highly flammable material that would have boosted the fire several times over.

Josef's second point was that the fire had been centred upon the very area that was designated for the production of Alirach. Was this the work of someone, possibly a jealous competitor, who wanted Alirach out of the way?

"Well, you may have a good point there, Josef, because my first thoughts were, could this have anything to do with Peter?" asked Alistair. "He had to back down over the patent rights issue, so I wonder if he is upset enough to want to inflict further damage?"

Josef admitted that this could be a possibility, but of course, he didn't know Peter very well and wasn't really in a position to add anything further, but equally, he felt that it might have a connection. However, there was one factor that might just help with identifying how the fire started. At the beginning of the fitting of CCTV units, Josef had one particular camera placed at the entrance and fairly hidden by foliage. This, in fact, was the first camera siting and it was a timed unit that swept the factory from one side to the other. It operated on a loop system that provided 24/7 coverage for a week. This was then downloaded to a central storage, and the camera then started a new filming for the next seven days. So, the pair left the fire-ridden area and walked back to Josef's office at the opposite end of the building, where the CCTV storage was located.

Although now fairly elderly as far as surveillance equipment goes, this CCTV camera still worked well and produced a clear definition. Josef set the storage to show what, if anything, was around over the period when the fire started. There was also a facility to switch to infra-red or night mode, depending upon the form you wanted the image to take. For what seemed like an eternity, nothing looked out of place. The weather conditions were dry with a gentle breeze moving the branches on the visible trees.

But then, in the far corner of the screen, a figure appeared, having scaled the fence that surrounded the factory. Although at some distance, the person was still relatively clear, and was carrying some form of bag or holdall, it was not easy to make out if the figure was male or female. Whoever it was then ran across to the factory and round to the rear of the building and out of the vision of the CCTV.

"I know that I wondered about the possibility that Peter could be involved, but I cannot tell if the person in this TV footage is him or not. When Rachel comes over tomorrow, she should have a look at it, too," said Alistair.

The following day the archival footage was once again run so that Rachel could also comment. At the clearest point of showing the figure, Josef increased the magnification as far as he could. At this point Rachel gave an intake of breath and exclaimed, "That's Peter!"

"But you can't see his face – how can you be so sure?" asked Alistair.

"Just look at the bobble hat that he's wearing. I gave him that for his birthday. It had exactly the same wavy blue band all the way round. It's too much of a coincidence that someone else is wearing the same one," said Rachel, "especially when the area that was being centred on was the production site for Alirach!"

"But we must wait for a while," said Josef. "There must be more footage if the intruder leaves in the same way that he entered."

Sure enough, CCTV did show the same person leaving by the same route that he had come into the factory. But this time, he was facing the camera full on and there was no mistaking that the guy in this picture was Peter Denhill.

In total agreement they decided that the police would be called in and as much evidence as they could gather would be passed on, particularly the CCTV footage. After meetings with fire officers, the insurance agent and the police, Josef was allowed to section off the Alirach production section so that he could return to working on his other projects. Meanwhile, the fire investigations continued and liaison with UK police as to the whereabouts of Peter Denhill was underway.

Chapter 11

Back home in North Devon, Alistair and Rachel still struggled to believe that Peter was behind the attempts to either steal the patent or destroy the factory. Rachel was particularly angry as she had pretty well always trusted Peter, and Alistair felt the same betrayal of trust as so much information had been taken or copied by Peter. But there was still much to do, even though the production of Alirach had stopped for the time being, and Rachel busied herself with the creating of Instruction Manuals, advertising literature and the building up of potential clients. Her lists seemed endless. The potential clients formed sub-divisions under the headings of Private Owners, Hire Companies, Boatyards, Holiday Cruise Companies, Commercial Cargo Companies, Shipping Lines, etc.

Still continuing with her coastal survey work, Rachel could only work on the Alirach project during evenings and weekends. Alistair was still trying to catch up with the garage backlog that had built up over the last few months. Although he had taken on a local mechanic in a full-time role, there was more than enough to keep him really busy. However, his mind still revolved around the past few months, searching for anything that might help unearth the reason why Peter should behave in this manner, as he was pretty sure that he was behind it. What Alistair couldn't understand was what was the ultimate gain for Peter? Did he want to get rid of Alirach because he couldn't get his hands on the patent? Was this a strange sort of revenge, or had he simply lost his mind? Unable to make sense of it, Alistair decided that the best policy was to let the police deal with it – plus, it could take a very long time before it all unravelled.

Josef and Daniel finally were able to have that part of their factory 'returned' to them as the fire inspectors left. The insurance company was satisfied that this was a legitimate claim and agreed on a settlement – not quite what Josef would have liked, but still enough to cover most of the loss incurred. What could be salvaged was cleaned and carefully checked before being put back into use where possible. Builders and decorators were brought in to clear out the debris and put the fire ridden area back ready to begin production again. During the time that the factory was out of use, Josef had maintained contact with his customers – the majority were sympathetic and agreed to the forced delay with their orders. A few decided that they couldn't wait and moved their orders to competitor companies. Josef knew that this could happen and, of course, had to accept this outcome. There was a little further help when Josef discovered that there was a payment by the insurance company for loss of profits. It was not large but nevertheless helped with the cost of restoring the business back to normal.

Whilst the builders and decorators were busy making good, Josef and Daniel travelled to North Devon for a meeting with Alistair and Rachel. The purpose of this was to decide the marketing strategy, finalise the sales literature and instruction manuals and tie up any loose ends that still needed attention. Josef explained how he distributed his products and suggested that some of these outlets could also be a marketing target for Alirach. As there was the potential for a really large customer base, they agreed that there should be selected group areas for their sales campaign. There would be a selected distributorship for the larger vessels, another for the boatyards building intermediate and smaller vessels, one that could specialise in companies that hired out motorboats and another that would deal with retrofit units to individual customers. By doing this they would be able to determine in which particular area (if any) produced the best growth. The Alirach turbine was pretty standard in the way it functioned. Still, there were variations in dimensions, which determined the output so far as the amount of electricity available was concerned.

Before Josef and Daniel returned to Switzerland, Alistair checked with his police contact if there was any further news about Peter Denhill. The reply suggested that something had taken their attention, but they currently could not divulge anything more concrete than that.

The next few weeks passed without anything other than the normal routine for Alistair and Rachel. The changeover in Switzerland was more than just routine as the production area for Alirach was almost ready to run. Daniel started on his visits to potential Alirach distributors whilst Josef supervised the factory. Rachel was planning to work out her strategy for UK distributor companies. Still, she had to put this on hold as she received a text from her coastal survey company asking her to make a trip to Northumberland as there were some problems that urgently needed sorting out.

Chapter 12

But two days after she had left, Alistair was completely taken by surprise as a knock on his door revealed a visit from Peter Denhill.

"I do hope that you will invite me in?" said Peter.

Still unable to arrange his thoughts, Alistair simply indicated that he should go through, closed the door and followed him into the lounge. But this short walk was enough for him to switch to sizing up what had just happened. He realised that Peter must have some idea that Alistair would hold him responsible for recent events, but then he wouldn't just walk into his house without some plan – and doubtless, it would not be in Alistair's favour.

"I'm sure that I am the last person that you expected to see, but I felt that it would be better for you to hear from me in person than by text or email. What I am going to ask you is very easy for you to do. I need to have an agreement in writing that you will arrange for me to receive 20% of the profit of every Alirach sold. This will be paid into an account in one of the major banks – details will be forwarded once I have your agreement in writing. I want the agreement sent by courier to an address that you will receive later this evening. I shall require this before the end of this week. Now I shall bid you good day." said Peter.

As Peter opened the door to leave, Alistair simply said, "That will happen at the same time that Hell freezes over!"

Climbing into his car, Peter called back, "I would think again if I were you – you may not see Rachel for a long time." And drove off.

It took Alistair a few seconds to fully realise the threat that Peter had just made. Rachel – where was she? He immediately rang her mobile but got the usual "Sorry, I am unable to answer your call. Please leave a message, and I'll call you back." Then it hit Alistair – Peter had kidnapped Rachel, and he was now holding her ransom. Unbelievable! The whole 'emergency' that Rachel had been called to Northumberland to deal with had been set up by Peter. But would Peter ever really harm Rachel?

Positive thinking came back to Alistair, and he immediately called his contact with the police and explained just what had taken place. Luckily, he remembered that there would be a doorbell video of Peter that he could forward to the police. Plus, they would be able to track Rachel's mobile phone both via the signal and through the Find My tracker that Rachel had installed.

Alistair's next call was to Josef, who, after a short conversation told Alistair that Daniel would come over straightaway to give whatever assistance he could to Alistair.

The next few days dragged painfully on for Alistair and Daniel. They spent time with John Denhill trying to discover where Peter was likely to be, what friends or other relations could help – anything that could lead them to Rachel. More news arrived that did nothing to lift their spirits. Although the doorbell video did give the police a description of what Peter was wearing and the car type and registration number, it didn't produce any encouraging results. The car was a rental, and the name and address given to the rental company were false. Also, Rachel's mobile phone was tracked to a waste bin in Newcastle and was totally wrecked.

The deadline set by Peter for the receipt of the agreement was closing in. The police had advised Alistair to do nothing for the moment. They were checking the address that Peter had sent to Alistair, which had turned out to be a central mail point for the public to use. Here again, the name of the recipient who would collect the document was fictitious.

The police arrived to meet with Alistair and Daniel to talk about the next stage of this harrowing event. As much information as possible about Peter was being amassed by police experts. This type of kidnapping usually followed a pattern, and experience over many years had shown that there were certain steps to take that would help to diffuse potential problems before they arose. It was suggested that the next step would be that Peter would contact Alistair and demand that as he hadn't carried out Peter's request for the agreement to be despatched there would be one final chance before harm may come to Rachel.

This happened the same evening. An email from Peter said that if the agreement had not been despatched and received within the next 48 hours, then Alistair could expect the request to be dramatically changed. A direct link had been established between the police and Alistair, so this message was instantly relayed to them. What followed was intense checking of the source of the email – the ability to track down the time, place and from what equipment was fully possible with the sophisticated means available today.

Within the hour, Alistair learned that they had established that the email was sent from a landline in a small village north of Newcastle. The intention was to pay an unannounced visit to this location and ask a few questions – if anyone was still there.

Yet again, Peter seemed to be ahead of the game. The property was empty, but the telephone landline was working, and it was soon shown to have been used to send the email to Alistair. Fingerprints didn't exist as the phone had been well-cleaned. Little evidence was around to show if anyone had actually lived there for a while. No food in the cupboards or empty fridge, and dust is accumulating in most places. Surprisingly, both the front and rear doors were unlocked.

Alistair and Daniel were becoming more and more concerned for Rachel. Alistair still felt that Peter wouldn't harm Rachel, but his track record over the recent past was equally confusing. If Alistair did nothing and made no response to Peter, what could he expect him to do next?

Further discussions took place with the police who had now set up a communications vehicle in Alistair's driveway and linked into his telephone network. They told Alistair and Daniel that they had been researching the background of Peter Denhill, talking to friends, relations, neighbours, and people he had worked for and with previously to gain as much knowledge as they possibly could. They had alerted various police forces in and around Newcastle, providing details and photos that might trigger a response.

The feeling was that if Peter got wind of the fact that there was a national search for him and Rachel taking place, then it was possible that he might abandon whatever plans he was making. If there was no further response by Alistair to Peter's attempt at getting an agreement for money from the sales of Alirach, then maybe he would think again about his future on the run.

But Alistair and Daniel were not so sure. They were becoming increasingly worried for Rachel. They argued that they would be happy to agree to forwarding the document that Peter wanted, have Rachel returned safely and deal with Peter after that. Once Rachel was home, they simply need not make any payments to Peter. Why wouldn't that work?

The police, however, felt that Peter would have already thought about this and may well have a second plan to ensure that after he let Rachel go, he would still be a recipient of income from Alirach. Just what this would entail, of course, wasn't known. But Alistair's suggestion seemed too easy to be the best way out of this mess, and Peter had proved that so far, he was one step ahead at each turn.

Eventually it was agreed, although somewhat reluctantly by Alistair and Daniel, that nothing should be done and they would wait to hear from Peter. The main point made by the police was that it was unlikely that any harm would come to Rachel, as without her, Peter had no bargaining power. At some stage, he must realise that the hunt for both him and Rachel would go on and on, and certainly whilst he was still making demands. If any harm came to Rachel, the penalty on Peter's head would increase tremendously, and the hunt for him would be more intense.

Chapter 13

The next communication from Peter arrived by email. Once again, the police were immediately tracking the source, to pinpoint just where Peter was hiding. This time, the message was a straightforward, if somewhat old-fashioned, ransom note. "I want you to arrange for £50,000 to be placed in the following bank account. This transfer must be completed within the next forty-eight hours. When I have proof of this, Rachel will be free to return."

Alistair knew that he just hadn't got that amount of available money to transfer within that time zone, but Daniel immediately said to Alistair that if he wanted to do this, he could arrange for that amount of money to be moved as requested. Once again, the police wanted to wait on making any decision whilst they were discovering where the email was coming from.

This time, the transmission of the email was shown to have come from a small hotel on the outskirts of Edinburgh. Police Scotland were given the data on Peter and quickly dispatched officers to the hotel in question. Once more, Alistair and Daniel had to wait, unable to do anything but let the law take the lead. Whatever they did to keep their minds away from thinking about Rachel's situation was never really going to work.

Alistair knew Peter much better than Daniel and tried to reassure him that he doubted that Peter would really harm Rachel. Currently clever enough to outwit his pursuers, Alistair knew that Peter was reasonably bright, but he also hoped that he would eventually understand that he was never going to win and that the odds were stacked against him. If he did think along these lines, then it may just prevent any real harm from coming to Rachel.

Finally, the police reported back on their visit to the hotel near Edinburgh. Although Peter was not there, the Receptionist did confirm that a man appearing to fit Peter's description had indeed booked a room that previous evening and had paid in advance – cash. She was unable to offer anything further other than a mobile number that she had been given as a contact for him. The booking was under the name of William Smith, and the address given was a false one in Glasgow. The mobile number appears to ring as a normal mobile but is not being answered. Again, checking the details of the mobiles that Peter used was becoming routine. This one was a pay-as-you-go cell phone, relatively inexpensive and would probably be found in a bin somewhere. The only difference with this one was that it was still ringing out when dialled. Did this mean that it was still being used and simply lying around somewhere? The location of this phone suddenly seemed important.

The location turned out to be at a property in the village of Oxley, some twenty miles south-east of Edinburgh. Further checking revealed that it was a holiday let owned by a local farmer who previously used it as the home for his stockman who had since retired. Enquiries showed that it had been currently booked for a four-week period by a man who claimed that he was doing a rural survey on migratory birds in this part of Scotland.

"I can't say what his movements are" said the farmer, "but he is backwards and forwards quite frequently. There may be someone else there as I have heard raised voices when I was repairing the fence at the back of the cottage. Other than that, I can't tell you anything more.

He did pay me cash up front for the month, so I can't complain, and as far as I know, he is still around."

This looked like a lead at last, and the police decided that they would post a continuous watch, day and night, from a selected vantage point. In order to maintain as much secrecy as possible, Alistair and Daniel were given a 'filtered' version of what the police were planning. If there was a chance that they could find Peter and Rachel in this cottage, then the fewer people who knew of this, the greater their chances of concluding the operation by surprise.

But a phone call from the farmer gave the police an opportunity to do something positive. Apparently, a leak had appeared in the cottage kitchen, and the farmer was asked if he could get it repaired as quickly as possible. The farmer also said that the guy would be away the next day, so could he have it done during that time?

This was the opportunity that the police were waiting for. With the agreement of the farmer, they arranged for a plumber to fix the leak and at the same time, they had their own experts position hidden cameras in strategic parts of the cottage and externally. All cameras were linked to police laptops and the local station. The next twenty-four hours should tell them just who is currently using the cottage and, with luck, confirm their suspicions.

Around 10.15 a.m. the following morning, the duty officer, observing the police laptop connected to the cottage cameras, rang his boss to tell him that the cameras were live and there were two characters moving around in the cottage. All relevant units were alerted and put on standby, waiting for the word to move in. Suspicions were correct as both Peter and Rachel could be clearly seen inside the cottage. Plans were drawn up as to how the police would surround the area and be prepared to call in unannounced.

But before anything else took place, all screens went dead. No pictures were being transmitted, and all cameras seemed to have been switched off. The officer in charge waited – checking that this was possibly a network failure or a simple transmission glitch that might just clear itself. But after several minutes, he decided that they would move in, albeit cautiously, having no wish to alert Peter that they knew he was there.

It took some fifteen minutes to reach the outskirts of the cottage, where they parked discreetly at some short distance from the entrance gateway. There was an estate vehicle parked in the driveway – hopefully denoting that Peter and Rachel were still inside. Slowly moving in, the police team surrounded the cottage, and once in position, the officer in charge knocked on the door.

Silence. No footsteps, no voices, not one sound from inside. The officer tried the door, which proved to be unlocked, and made his way in, followed by more officers. Total silence. Even though the possibility of Peter and Rachel hiding somewhere crossed his mind, the officer knew that they were no longer in the cottage. A full search proved that the place was empty. Unless they had another vehicle, Peter and Rachel must have left on foot. Further inspection of the cameras provided sufficient proof that Peter had discovered their whereabouts and shut down the transmission link.

Although highly disappointed, the officer in charge reported back to Headquarters, who would now take over the operation. A decision was made to activate the police helicopter and comb the area, checking on the possibility that they may still be on foot, although not really likely given the local terrain. Photos of Peter and Rachel were distributed to all police stations and sub-stations in the surrounding areas, and similar details were forwarded to rail and bus stations, airports and ferry terminals.

If they did have another vehicle, it would be even harder to guess which direction they would take. All the major car hire companies had been alerted. Again, it was not possible to be sure that some of the smaller ones were on their list.

Chapter 14

Alistair and Daniel had been told of the situation so far. They both agreed that it was some relief to know that Rachel was still okay, so far as it could be reported. What they were concerned about was the next communication from Peter. What would he now ask for? He was very obviously aware of the fact that he was being 'hunted' by the police and that, so far, none of his requests had been granted. Would this cause him to think along more drastic lines in getting what he wanted? It seemed clear that he was only after money, but also he must now feel that his chances of actually getting any were reducing. Would this make him more dangerous, more reckless? These thoughts did not sit well with Alistair, who stopped trying to work out how Peter was now going to react.

It was 2.20 a.m., a time that Alistair would never forget for the rest of his life. His phone rang, and Alistair felt that it just had to be Peter with his next demands. He picked it up and waited. A voice said, "Hello, Dad!"

Sitting around the table with the officer in charge of this operation, Alistair explained what he had heard from Rachel in that early phone call. She was initially fine and told Alistair that she had not been treated badly by Peter and had managed to keep her spirits up despite the trauma that was happening. As she explained the current situation, her emotions began to take over, and she was close to tears. All the time she was being held hostage by Peter she had maintained a belief that at some point Peter would make a mistake and she would see her chance to get away.

However, he seemed to be constantly watching his back and rarely left Rachel out of his sight. But the first error that he made was with the mobile phone that the police had traced to the cottage. Rachel found it on the floor of the cottage kitchen, partly hidden by a scruffy mat and quickly hid it. Previous phones, including her own, had been destroyed and disposed of by Peter, but for some reason, he appeared to have either forgotten about this one or maybe even thought he had already got rid of it. This was more of a possibility when Rachel realised that he was already using another one, which gave her the hope that she now had the means to ask for help.

Rachel knew that the only time she could use the phone was when she was absolutely certain that Peter could not possibly hear her making a call. This really meant during the night, when she was locked in her room and could try to phone under the bed covers to mute the sound, which is just what she did when she rang Alistair. Alistair then explained to Rachel that it might be safest if she switched the mobile phone to silent mode and that the next contact that he would make would be by text message and so be soundless. He asked her to keep the phone on so that the police could track it. Also, when it was safe to do so, she could try to text their whereabouts each time Peter moved them on. Above all, do not take risks.

All agreed that Alistair had done the right thing, and for Rachel's sake, there must be no mistakes when using this phone. The police continued monitoring the whereabouts of Rachel's newly acquired cell phone and logging all details of the route that Peter was taking. They knew that he wouldn't be contacting his grandfather, but they had no information of any friends or contacts that he may have in Scotland.

A potential lead about the vehicle that Peter may have rented came to light when a small car hire firm in Dalkeith contacted the police to say that a man fitting Peter's description had hired a blue diesel Peugeot from them a couple of days ago. He had taken it for one week and paid cash when he collected it. They gave the registration number together with what could be a false name and residential address if it was Peter who hired it. These details were circulated to police covering the area in which the mobile phone that Rachel had was being tracked.

For a while, things were quiet. Nothing further from Rachel, and Alistair felt that they did not want to make unnecessary contact with each other for fear of Peter finding Rachel with the phone. They were, however, expecting to hear from Peter, which they felt would be 'good' news insomuch that he was still keeping contact.

Meanwhile, the police were carefully tracking Rachel's mobile phone and were now following it as it moved in a westerly direction somewhere between Livingston and Glasgow. The outline plan was to have unmarked police cars driving along the potential route that Peter seemed to be taking and looking out for the blue Peugeot. If the phone tracking did match up to be in the same position as the blue Peugeot, then this may just be the answer they wanted.

Now, it was back to a waiting game. Trying to guess where Peter was going and what he was likely to do next was like looking for the proverbial needle in a haystack. It was unlikely that Alistair would hear from Rachel until sometime during the night, as the risk of Peter discovering her secret phone was far too great. But he also knew that this hostage-taking had to end very soon – certainly before Peter had time to consider something that might be more threatening to Rachel.

The deadline that Peter had set for the transfer of £50,000 had passed, and Alistair was waiting for whatever Peter had planned next. A text message arrived just before 11.00 p.m. that evening. It simply said – "You failed to make the payment by the set time. The amount now will be set at £80,000, and this is my last demand. If you really want Rachel back, I suggest that you do not ignore this request and transfer the money within the next forty-eight hours."

This text was also picked up by the duty officer through the link with Alistair's phone. Immediately, the tracking system was activated, and Peter's destination would soon become apparent. The operations team also engaged the tracker with Rachel's phone and compared the coordinates.

They matched. They now had a pinpoint destination for Peter, and plans were quickly established to arrange for a visit. Again, it followed the previous pattern where Peter had opted for a small, none-too-conspicuous hotel, this time just outside Glasgow. At a few minutes passed midnight, Alistair received a text from Rachel. It simply said, "At the Camelot Hotel, on A72 outside Larkhall. I'm OK - xx"

Chapter 15

All details were now with the police, and all Alistair and Daniel could do was wait – and worry. They assumed that the police would send in a trained squad to surround the hotel, gain entry and relieve Peter of his precious hostage. But he had eluded them before, and until they had word from Larkhall that all had gone to plan, they could do nothing.

The first piece of information that Alistair and Daniel received from the police was that sitting in the car park of the hotel was a blue Peugeot Estate with the same registration number that they had been given by the car hire company in Dalkeith. Surely this must be the end for Peter?

The plan by the police squad near the hotel was based on almost total secrecy. Contact had been made with the owner – who was also the Receptionist of this small hotel – and it was established that Peter (under yet another name) and his guest had taken two rooms for three nights. Yet again, the rooms had been paid for in cash. The room numbers were given to the police, and arrangements were made that allowed the police to make their own entry at some point during that night.

How they would approach Peter was discussed in great detail. There were two potential plans under scrutiny. The first was to enter the hotel during the early hours and enter Peter's room as quickly and quietly as possible or to text Rachel and ask her to go to bed dressed to go out and wait for the police to collect her and leave the hotel as discreetly as possible. Then they would pay a visit to Peter's room and introduce themselves.

It was decided that getting Rachel out of the hotel would be the priority, so a text was sent letting her know the time that they would be coming to her room and then taking her to safety. Once again, it was a waiting game.

Alistair and Daniel were kept in the picture by the police, but for obvious reasons, not all the details were relayed to them, just enough to let them know that they were progressing in the way that they had planned. Both of them longed to make contact with Rachel via her mobile, but they also knew that this could jeopardise the operation if Peter found out.

At the agreed time, the police entered the Camelot Hotel and made their way to Rachel's room. Luckily, it was not directly opposite Peter's room but a little further along the corridor. They opened the door and entered. Rachel was under the bed covers and fully dressed. The officer in charge whispered to Rachel that they would quietly exit the hotel and walk a short distance to the waiting police cars.

The plan worked well – no sounds were heard from Peter's room as they passed his door, and there was no one around as they walked to the police car. The car left and drove to Glasgow Central Police Station. It was from here that Rachel rang Alistair and Daniel.

At Camelot Hotel the second part of the operation was about to get underway. The hotel was silently surrounded by police, and three officers approached Peter's room. They quietly unlocked the door and entered with the greeting, "Good Morning Mr. Denhill, we have come to take you for breakfast!" but then realised that this was spoken to an empty room. Not a sign of Peter. Bed made, clothes gone – almost as if the room had never been occupied. A double-check with the owner that this was the correct room, and they soon realised that Peter had, yet again, been one step ahead – but this time without his hostage. Although they searched the hotel with a fine toothcomb – it was possible that Peter may have tried to hide in the hotel until they had left – they did find evidence that the rear fire door had been opened from the inside but was not closed again from the outside. Peter had made his escape, but without his current hire vehicle, which was still parked at the front of the hotel, and without his hostage and no bargaining power.

An alert was immediately put out on the police network, but this time only for Peter. They assumed that he had left on foot, and local vehicle hire companies were again circulated with his details.

Needless to say, the reunion with Alistair and Daniel was an enormous relief for the three of them. Despite her ordeal, Rachel was in better shape than Alistair expected. She was so angry with Peter, and this helped her to pass her time as a hostage by constantly thinking of ways to escape. Even to the extent of causing Peter physical harm if it came to it – something that surprised Alistair, but not that he would have been against it had it taken place. Rest and the return to her normal life were all that Rachel wanted. In fact, the first thing she said to Daniel when they met on her return from Scotland was, "How is Alirach going?"

The police asked for a debriefing to discuss what had taken place over the last several days and what they planned for the future so far as Peter was concerned. They were conscious that Peter had outwitted them on more than one occasion and may well still have reasons for not leaving Alistair and Rachel alone. New safety measures would be put in place to offer further protection for them. They were still not sure how Peter had got wind of their visit to the hotel at Larkhall, but somehow, he knew they were there, but with insufficient time to take

Rachel with him. This may have shaken his confidence as he now had nothing to bargain with and may well be running out of funds.

Returning to their routine roles, Alistair Rachel and Daniel began to live their lives with much easier minds. They were aware that Peter was still at large, but they really did not believe that he would try anything more as he must know that there would be extra security in place. Also, as he knew only too well, there would be no reason to consider Alirach as a means to get him money.

Rachel had arranged with her company to be able to work from home for a period rather than risk the potential threat from Peter by travelling to work each day. This obviously pleased Alistair as he could keep an eye on Rachel.

In Switzerland the trials with mobile Alirach had gone really well, and production had already produced the first run for commercial sales. Josef had obviously kept in regular touch with Daniel and Alistair, and he was delighted that no harm had come to Rachel. It looked as though there was some 'normality' in place, and life could resume without stress or trauma.

Chapter 16

One evening, fairly late on, Alistair received a text. It read, "Don't think that this is over – you will regret not paying me as you were required to. Wait for new instructions." Even though there was no signature, it was obviously from Peter. Alistair forwarded it straight to the police but, for the moment, decided not to say anything to Rachel. Just when things looked to be getting back on track, thought Alistair. He also wondered if Peter was actually losing his mind, and what had seemed to him to be a way of making some quick money was now turning into an obsession. Despite receiving this text, Alistair felt that there was no way that Peter could cause further damage as they had the full force of the police behind them.

For the next few days, nothing came from Peter, but there was an update from the police. They had traced the text provider to a location outside Bristol – to what appeared to be a house, not a hotel or pub. Local police were combing the area but no alerts had been issued yet, and no contact with car hire firms. They wanted to have a sighting or some form of proof that it was Peter before they proceeded with any further action.

This did worry Alistair as Bristol was within striking distance of his home, and that started him thinking about what could Peter do, to extract money from him without a reason – or a hostage? I need to stop trying to work out what he will try next and simply concentrate on my work. So that is what he did.

Sitting in the small lounge in the cottage that he had rented, Peter was trying to work out his next move. He was running out of money, having spent a small fortune on hotels, hire cars, mobile phones and food. He had realised that he was being tracked via the mobile phone and had purchased several cheap pay-as-you-go phones and discarded them every time he called Alistair. But he also remembered that the reason that the police tracked him to the hotel at Larkhall was that he had not disposed of the phone he used at Oxley and that Rachel must have found it and had contacted the police. So now he would get rid of the phone each time he called Alistair, and hopefully, there would be no way of tracking him.

He decided that there was another problem with hiring cars as they, too, could be tracked if his details had been circulated. Although money was dwindling, he made up his mind to buy an elderly but still roadworthy vehicle. To make things less conspicuous, his choice would be based on something that was around the roads every day and in a popular colour. He ended up with a blue Ford Fiesta, which he felt would blend in with traffic without causing attention. So now he was all set to pay a visit to Mr Alistair Andersen.

His first stop was to shop to pick up the provisions he needed for the next few days. He had decided that he would camp out rather than pay for accommodation. He found a camping shop and equipped himself with a tent, sleeping bag and other basic essentials required for a few nights in the open air. Feeling pleased with his shopping and clearer about his next move, Peter set off for Alistair's house. But he was so tied up in his thoughts that he was completely taken by surprise by what happened next.

A car appeared in his rear-view mirror, which was not unusual, but this one suddenly switched on blue flashing lights and a police siren. He was signalled to pull over onto the hard shoulder with an obvious request to stop. His mind was racing. *What have I missed? How do they know it's me?*

"Good morning, sir? Could you switch the engine off, please?" Peter did as he was told and got out to stand on the passenger side of the unmarked police car with the police officer. Was this it? Is it all over? Panic was starting to take over.

"Do you know why I have stopped you?" asked the officer.

"I really have no idea," said Peter.

"Then I assume you have missed the fact that you are in a restricted speed area as your speed was shown to be in excess of 65 m.p.h. and this is a designated 50 m.p.h. Speed zone," replied the officer.

"Aah!" exclaimed Peter, with a slight feeling of relief. "Yes, I have certainly missed the sign. Otherwise, I would have been travelling at a slower speed. I do apologise, officer."

"I need your details, sir. Do you have your driving licence with you?" asked the policeman.

Peter suddenly froze. He was aware that he had committed a speeding offence, but if he gave his details it would certainly get back to those police who were looking for him. This officer didn't seem to be concerned about who he was – just a driver who had broken the law. But could he risk giving out information which will provide the police once more of his whereabouts.

"Ah, yes – I'll get it from the car," replied Peter. The officer waited whilst Peter walked round and got into the driving seat. Whilst delving into the dashboard with a show of getting his driving licence, he managed to fasten his seat belt, then slamming his door, took off at speed.

The stunned officer realised that there was more to this than just a speeding offence. As he raced after the blue Fiesta, he reported what had just taken place, including a description of both Peter, the car and the registration number. The reply came back somewhat surprised the officer as he was told that he was not to stop Peter but to follow him from a safe distance away. They wanted Peter to think that he had managed to elude the unmarked police car and simply wanted to know where he was going.

The tactics changed as the police decided to switch the unmarked police car for another one that would not be recognised by Peter. The plan was for the second car to take over at some stage and continue to discreetly follow Peter, who would soon think he had outwitted the police car – they hoped.

As he drove, Peter thought about what had just happened. He may be free to go wherever he wanted at the moment, but he knew that this car was now a target for the police, who had the registration number and a description of both him and the car. He would have to dump this one and find another, and fast. What chance had he got of doing this within the next half-hour? It also struck him that the unmarked police car could have easily overtaken him and forced him to stop – but it didn't. So he deduced that they were following him to find out his intended destination. Then what? Perhaps the best thing for Peter was to 'lose' the unmarked car as quickly as possible and give himself more time to work out the next phase. He had been driving in fairly heavy traffic for a while, but despite regularly checking, he could no longer see the unmarked police car in his mirror. A little further up the road, he spotted a layby with two fuel tankers parked. As he approached he saw that he would be able to park in a small space between the two, helping to make him less noticeable as the traffic passed by. Believing that this was worth the risk, he did just that, and they watched the traffic as they drove past. After some minutes, the unmarked car that had stopped him for speeding drove past, and Peter waited a while before pulling out and continuing his journey.

Chapter 17

Peter had become a risk-taker this last week or so, and he decided that he would take some more to get out of the current situation. Time was moving on, and a new plan was forming in his head. Using his phone he located a scrap yard in the next town and paid it a visit. Finding someone to help him, he explained that his nephew had built himself a large pedal car out of bits and pieces. Peter wanted to help him, and the nephew asked if he could have a proper steering wheel and a pair of number plates to make it look real. The scrapyard man told Peter to look in the store, and he may find something there. Peter dug around, found a steering wheel and picked up four number plates. He explained that by juggling the letters and numbers around, he could come up with his nephew's age and month of birth. The guy agreed, and Peter left with his findings.

What he had actually done when picking the number plates was to select ones that had appropriate numbers and letters he could put on the Fiesta. Next he looked and found a suitable remote spot where he could switch the plates over and so give himself a little more time before he needed another form of transport.

What he now wanted was to find a small campsite where he could set up for one night and finalise his plan. What looked like a suitable spot he came across near Burnham-on-Sea. It was somewhat run down and scruffy but did have a few tents in residence. Peter thought it would suit him well as his car would not look out of place alongside the others parked there. The man who took his money was far more interested in talking on his phone and told Peter he could pitch wherever suited him best. So he set up his tent in the far corner of the site, almost hidden from the main entrance. Then, he worked on his plan for the next couple of days.

The campsite was roughly four hundred yards from a beach, and the following morning, Peter took himself off for a walk along the coast. Thinking of all the things he could do to extract some worthwhile amount of money out of Alistair he was slowly developing a new plan. After around an hour or so he returned to his campsite feeling more positive about his next moves. He noticed that two of the tents that were closest to him had gone while he was out. A little more privacy, he thought. But his thoughts soon changed when he opened up his tent.

Empty – just about everything was gone. He went straight to his car and found it had a side window smashed, and pretty much everything had been taken. His mind raced. Was it to do with the two tents that had left the site, or had Alistair something to do with it? Panic struck. What was to do next? He had little money, no spare mobile phones apart from the one in his pocket, and was left with no food, camping equipment or spare clothes. The only thing he could think of was to throw himself at the mercy of his Uncle, John Denhill. It was a long shot, but Peter was beginning to feel more and more desperate. The thought of handing himself into the police terrified him. So he patched up the car window as best he could, loaded up what was left of his possessions and headed for his Uncle's farm.

Thoughts were constantly buzzing around Peter's head as he drove along the M5. Could he talk to Rachel? Could he persuade her that he had made a massive mistake, and would she forgive him for putting her through so much trauma? Would Alistair and Daniel understand that it was never directed at them personally? Tears of frustration and helplessness were forming, and his head was starting to hurt with innumerable images forming. Then, without warning, everything went black.

Peter would never know what happened. Three drivers had given their individual accounts of what had taken place to the police, and all three had formed the same conclusion.

Chapter 18

Sitting in Alistair's lounge, along with Rachel and Daniel, the officer who had been in charge of this case from the start was explaining how Peter had died in a road traffic accident on the northbound carriageway of the M5 south of Bristol.

"He was travelling south at some speed when his car began veering across the carriageway before hitting the central reservation safety fencing, rolling over into the fast lane of the northbound carriageway and into the path of an oncoming fuel tanker. It would have been an instant end for Peter – the car was totally wrecked." explained the officer. The three were stunned at this report.

"I have to ask – but this was a genuine accident and not deliberate by Peter, do you think?" asked Alistair.

"So far as we can determine from the statements of the drivers following Peter and from the road markings that we have examined, the car became erratic in behaviour, but we found no evidence of heavy braking or tyre marks at the scene. So, currently, we are left without a positive answer, and because of the extensive damage to the car it will be some time before we can discover if there were any defects that would contribute further information about this crash." the officer replied.

The atmosphere that evening was of great sadness and felt by all three despite the actions that Peter had inflicted on them. It wasn't much consolation that finally it was over, and there would be no long court case to deal with whilst everything was dragged up and re-lived. It would be something that would never be forgotten but would always remain at the back of their minds, more so for Rachel than the others. The only conclusion that they came to was that Peter had taken up the idea, for some reason, that he wanted revenge for not getting more financial reward for his part in Alirach. Other than that, he must have been slowly losing his mind, as his actions were certainly not rational.

They returned to their respective roles but with one big change. Alirach sales were steadily increasing, both in the U.K. and overseas. Because of this, Rachel left her job and started working full-time with Alirach. Her relationship with Daniel flourished, and it wasn't long before their engagement was announced. Naturally, both Alistair and Josef were delighted.

On an evening, as the sun was about to disappear, Rachel and Alistair were sitting in their garden before going in for supper.

"I've been thinking," said Rachel, " before you finally retire, Dad, there's just one more job that I would like your help with."

"As long as it is legal, simple and requires the minimum of effort, then I'll consider it!" laughed Alistair.

"Oh, it's all of those," replied Rachel, " just to design an Alirach that we put under the sea to turn the tide!"

****

www.ingramcontent.com/pod-product-compliance
Lightning Source LLC
Chambersburg PA
CBHW040332020826
48978CB00013BC/1265